PETB🐾TS

Having illustrated numerous children's books, Judy Brown thought it was about time that she wrote some of her own. *Petbots* is her third and latest series of children's novels.

Judy has three children and lives in Surrey with her family and cats.

You can find out all about her at www.judybrown.co.uk.

PETB🐱TS

THE GREAT
ESCAPE

JUDY BROWN

Piccadilly

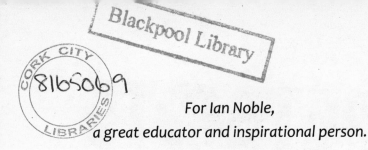

For Ian Noble,
a great educator and inspirational person.

First published in Great Britain in 2014
by Piccadilly Press,
A Templar/Bonnier publishing company
Deepdene Lodge, Deepdene Avenue,
Dorking, Surrey, RH5 4AT
www.piccadillypress.co.uk

A catalogue record for this book is available
from the British Library

ISBN: 978 1 84812 348 9

1 3 5 7 9 10 8 6 4 2

Printed in the UK by CPI Group (UK) Ltd, Croydon, CR0 4YY
Cover design by Simon Davis

Chapter 1

For Sale

'Well, I guess that's it,' said Archie. 'The Professor's not coming back.'

Archie the robot cat watched gloomily as a man wearing overalls attached a *For Sale* sign to the gatepost in front of the house. Archie's robot companions – Flo the bird and Sparky the mouse – joined him at the attic window.

'What are we going to do?' asked Flo.

'Good question,' said Archie.

Archie, Flo and Sparky had been living alone in the big house ever since Professor McVitie had been taken away in an ambulance six weeks

before. He was very old and quite frail, and the longer he was away, the more their fears grew.

'One thing I remember the Prof saying before he left,' said Archie, 'was that if he didn't come back, we should check the emergency file he left on the computer for instructions.'

'Well, what are we waiting for?' said Flo, leading the way out of the attic and down to the Professor's cluttered workshop in the basement. The three of them settled in front of the Professor's computer.

'Here it is,' said Archie, and clicked on a folder named *Goodbye Petbots.*

The Professor's friendly old face filled the screen. 'Petbots,' he began, 'if you're watching this, it looks like you're on your own.' He dabbed the corner of his eye with a handkerchief.

'Oh, Professor,' gasped Flo.

He went on. 'I've put together some little films to show how you were built from start to finish, so that if anything goes wrong or you breakdown, you will be able to fix each other. I've made a folder with blueprints, wiring diagrams, mechanics – everything you'll need to help keep yourselves in good repair now I'm gone. All the details are in my notebooks and I've labelled all the boxes in the workshop that have spare parts.' The Professor smiled broadly. 'You've looked after me well, Petbots. Now it's time to look after yourselves. Goodbye and good luck.'

The film clip ended.

Professor McVitie was an inventor. He'd often told the Petbots the story of how they came to be. The Professor had lived like a hermit in the big old house, and hardly ever went outside. He ordered everything he needed online – food, clothes, parts for his inventions – so there was no real reason for him to leave the house anyway. Besides, the Professor felt that any time away from his inventing was a waste of time. After a while, though, he began to get lonely and he decided he needed some company.

A dog would be out of question, of course – going for walks and throwing sticks wouldn't fit in with his busy inventing schedule – and he decided to get himself a cat instead, because cats are much more independent. So, on a rare trip out of the house, the Professor visited the local cat home, picked out a likely candidate from the feline inhabitants, filled out the relevant forms and took his new companion home.

It didn't go well.

Although he invented an ingenious automated cat biscuit dispenser to feed his new friend, it only worked when he remembered to fill it. Einstein the cat therefore began to look for food elsewhere. He became very popular with the

neighbourhood children, spending more and more time in their houses and less and less in his own. Eventually he just moved out. The Professor didn't even notice until the neighbours came to the house to bring Einstein back, but they all agreed that Einstein would be better off staying where he was.

'If only there was a pet that could look after itself completely,' said the Professor as he waved Einstein goodbye. 'One that didn't need feeding. One that could even help around the house . . . Wait a moment! That's it!' A brilliant idea flashed into the Professor's mind. 'Petbots!'

He stayed up all night working on plans and ideas, and by the morning, the first Petbot blueprint was finished.

9

Robot Cat 1. RC1 for short.

'Fantastic!' said the Professor. He'd found a way to combine his need for a companion with his skills as an inventor. He couldn't have been happier.

In the Professor's workshop, the Petbots were looking at the computer files that the Professor had left. One folder was labelled, *Start Here* and Archie clicked it open.

'That looks interesting,' said Archie, opening a file called *Video Diaries*.

It was a time-lapse film showing Archie's own construction – bolt by bolt, rivet by rivet, and circuit board by circuit board – made over a period of six weeks. When he was finally complete, the Professor flicked a switch and

Archie's eyes opened for the first time. To Archie, it felt a bit like watching himself being born.

'Awesome!' he said.

'Welcome to the world, RC!' said the Professor in the video clip. 'Ha, sounds like Archie! Well, Archie, I'm the Professor. It's lovely to meet you!'

From that day, Archie had been the Professor's constant companion, and soon after he was joined by Flo the bird – named after the Professor's favourite aunt – and Sparky the mouse, who got his name from the trail of sparks he left behind him when he was going at full speed. The Professor designed them all to have some special talents too.

Archie was in charge of the day-to-day running of the household, with the help of the others, of course. They did the washing, cleaning and cooking, and kept the Professor company when he was feeling lonely. He was very grateful to have

them looking after him, and they enjoyed making him happy. When he made a new invention, he would often show the Petbots first, and Archie even helped him out in the workshop now and then. He helped more and more as the Professor got older and his eyesight wasn't so good.

After the Professor went away, they kept up with their daily chores, making sure everything would be clean and tidy for him when he returned.

Archie monitored the Professor's email and correspondence and made sure the workshop machinery was all running smoothly. He and Flo checked the food supplies,

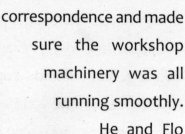

and Flo and Sparky made sure the house was in good repair, clean and dust free. They worked together, just as they always had, keeping things as they always had been, but now there was no Professor to care for, the Petbots began to wonder what would happen next. Looking after the Professor and the house was one thing, but would they really be able to look after themselves and everything else without him?

It was clear everything was going to change.

Chapter 2

An Uninvited Guest

'Does that sign mean that they're going to sell our home?' asked Flo. She'd flown over for a closer look at the *For Sale* sign while Archie and Sparky were doing their daily recharge of their solar-powered batteries in the sunny back garden. Flo landed back down next to them and spread out her wings so that her own panels could soak up the light.

'Yes, unfortunately, I think it does,' said Archie.

'Where will we go? What will we do? We'll be homeless!' squeaked Sparky.

'Don't worry, Sparky,' said Archie. 'We'll be okay.' But Archie really wasn't sure that they would be.

'What's that?' Archie's radar ears had picked up a sound from the front garden.

Flo flew up to the roof to take a look. 'It's a man with a clipboard and a camera,' she called down.

'Is he wearing a suit?' asked Archie.

'Why the sudden interest in fashion?' replied Flo.

'If he's in a suit, I'll bet he's an estate agent come to measure up the house and take photos.'

'That's bad, isn't it?' said Sparky.

'He's wearing a suit all right, and he's talking

into a digital recorder, saying things about the house,' said Flo, landing back in the garden.

'That's not good at all,' said Archie. 'We'd better keep an eye on him.'

Sparky got ready to speed off.

'Wait,' said Archie, 'we don't want him to see us. He might just chuck us out on the spot. And remember what the Professor used to say . . . If someone ever saw us and got hold of us, it's pretty likely we'd be dismantled to see how we work. The Professor was a genius. They'd stand no chance of figuring out how to put us back together.'

Flo shuddered.

They moved quietly to the back of the house. Archie extended his neck just enough to look through the kitchen window, trying to see where the estate agent was.

'There. He just went in the living room. I'll turn up my audio output so that we can all hear what he's saying.' Archie pressed a small button on his chest so that the sound came through his speakers.

'The house is a large Victorian residence in need of significant repair, updating and refurbishment,'

they heard the man say into his recorder. Then there was a click as he switched it off. 'What a dump,' he said. 'I'd justtear it all down and build some flats. You'd make a fortune on a plot like this.'

Flo looked horrified.

'How rude!' said Archie. 'That's our home he's insulting.'

The estate agent's mobile rang. 'Hi, Clive speaking. Yes, I'm here now. Bit of a goldmine, this one. Yes. About half an hour, I reckon. Okay, bye.'

The recorder clicked on again and they heard

Clive open the basement door – the door to the Professor's workshop. 'There is a substantial basement full of potential – and a load of old rubbish!' he chuckled, before moving through the rest of the house. 'The kitchen needs complete refurbishment but is large and airy.' They heard Clive move towards the staircase in the hall. 'Upstairs there are . . .'

'Quick, Flo, fly up and watch through the window and keep an eye on what he's doing,' said Archie.

'I'm going too!' said Sparky, and he zoomed up the drainpipe, leaving his customary trail of sparks. He zipped through the tiny gap in the bathroom window and hid behind the Professor's electric toothbrush, just as Clive came onto the landing.

Archie listened as Clive the estate agent walked from room to room making snide comments about the state of the place. Then he went up to their attic room. Sparky followed, darting here and there, silently and stealthily hiding behind various pieces of furniture. Flo watched from her perch on the window ledge outside.

'What's all this junk?' said Clive, kicking a box of nuts and bolts across the floor.

The house was crammed full of the Professor's various inventions, and Clive started shoving things about that were in his way. He laughed at the strange contraptions sitting around in the rooms upstairs, like the Mega-Maid – a four-armed dusting machine the Professor had built for Flo – the solar-powered Super Sucker vacuum, and the Amazing Stair Chair, which had helped the Professor get to the top landing in his later years.

'Seriously!' Clive chortled. 'What was this guy's problem?!'

Sparky followed him at a safe distance, getting crosser and crosser with the estate agent's behaviour.

'Ooops!' Clive knocked over a family photo of the Professor and his Petbots and it crashed to the floor, glass shattering everywhere.

That was the last straw.

Sparky zoomed right past Clive's ankles at full speed and circled around him fast enough to create a little dust cloud, before racing off at hyperspeed back into hiding.

Clive went pale. Little goose bumps came up all over him.

'Wha— What was that?' he said. 'Hello? Is somebody there?' He darted looks all around the

empty room, then shook his head hurriedly. 'Pull yourself together, Clive,' he told himself. 'It's just all this old stuff giving you silly ideas. It was probably just a draught . . . or something.'

Flo was falling about laughing on the window ledge.

After that, Clive did the fastest measuring job he'd ever done with a digital tape measure, but by the time he was finished, he'd pretty much talked himself out of being scared. 'Back to the office,' he mumbled. 'Think I'll make an appointment for the opticians this afternoon. I'm well overdue an eye test.' And so saying, he got back into his car and drove away.

The Petbots returned to the basement workshop.

'That was hilarious!' cackled Flo. 'He thought Sparky was a ghost!'

'Nasty, rude man,' said Sparky. 'He's lucky I didn't go up his trouser leg.'

'You know,' said Archie, 'we could work on that. The ghost idea, I mean. Who'd want to buy a haunted house? They'd leave this place alone then and we'd be safe.'

'You've got something there,' agreed Flo. She projected an action replay of Clive's reaction to

Sparky's prank and they all had a good laugh at Clive's expense.

'We'll need to be organised about this, though . . . Make a proper plan,' said Archie.

'And we'll need to be ready at a moment's notice,' said Flo. 'We won't know when he's going to turn up again.'

'Yes, that's true. It'll have to be timed like a military strategy,' Archie agreed, and wrote *Operation Ghost* on the whiteboard. 'We can use some of the Professor's inventions too. There's the remote-controlled lock on the door to the basement, from when he thought someone was stealing his ideas. I can do something with that.' He wrote the idea on the board.

'Oooh yes,' said Flo, 'and we can use the house's built-in sound system too.'

Archie wrote that down as well.

'Brilliant!' squealed Sparky. 'What can I do? What can I do?' he asked, bouncing up and down excitedly.

'Well, Sparky,' said Archie, thoughtfully, 'I've a special job in mind for you . . .'

Once they'd put all their ideas together, they divided the tasks between them. It was quite exciting to have something to focus on and they spent the rest of the day preparing the house for the next visit by Clive the estate agent. They couldn't wait to put their plans into action.

Chapter 3

Operation Ghost

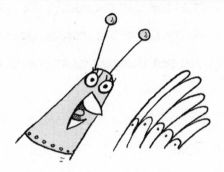

The Petbots didn't have long to wait. The following afternoon, Flo was on look-out duty when she spotted Clive's car approaching the house. She flapped her wings in excitement and flew down to tell Archie, who was in the kitchen checking everything was ready.

'Action stations!' said Flo.

'Okay, switch to internal communication so no one else will hear us. Positions, everybody! Let's give Clive a visit he'll never forget,' said Archie. 'Operation Ghost is officially go!'

Flo flew upstairs, Archie went to the basement control centre and Sparky waited patiently in the hallway.

The key turned in the front door lock and in came Clive, accompanied by a young couple.

'Come in, Mr and Mrs Bunting, come in and see the potential of this beautiful residence. A unique "doer-upper" opportunity, if ever I saw one.'

'It's a bit gloomy,' said Mrs Bunting, seemingly unimpressed with his sales patter.

'Ah, but just imagine the walls painted white – how bright and welcoming it would be!'

'I guess so . . .' she said vaguely.

Clive turned his attention to Mr Bunting. 'Let's start with the kitchen. The hub of the house!'

'Okay, activate phase one!' said Archie, who was watching on CCTV.

Sparky whizzed past the unwelcome visitors into the kitchen, up the wall and onto the shelf behind them, where all the pots and pans were kept. Clive was continuing with his sales pitch.

'There are some lovely original features in here – the high ceiling, the old range cooker, the sink and —'

CRASH!!!

A large metal saucepan clattered to the kitchen floor. Clive nearly jumped out of his skin.

'What the —?!' exclaimed Mr Bunting. Mrs Bunting was clinging to him as if her life depended on it.

'Oh, you know these old houses,' laughed Clive, nervously remembering his first visit to the house. 'Probably fell off a rusty old hook or something, ha ha.' A bead of sweat appeared on his forehead. 'Now, as you will see, the house has a substantial basement.'

But as Clive edged towards the half-open basement door, it suddenly slammed shut.

Downstairs, at the control centre, Archie started giggling.

Clive tried to open the door. 'Ha ha, er, just a draught, I'm sure,' he said in an attempt to convince himself as much as his clients. He tried turning the handle, but the door just wouldn't budge. 'Um, it seems to be stuck,' he said with a fixed grin. He rattled the handle and pushed the door with his shoulder. 'Ha ha, you know these —'

'— old houses?' said Mr Bunting, completing his sentence for him.

'Er, yes, quite!' Clive blushed. 'Let's have a look around upstairs,' he said. They walked back into the hall, all of them trying to ignore the fact that, as they did, the door to the basement slowly creaked open behind them.

'Upstairs, there are no less than five double bedrooms,' Clive continued, in a valiant attempt to ignore the growing fear that that the house was indeed haunted. 'Perfect for a growing family.'

'Did you hear that, darling? Tarquin and Jacintha could both have their own rooms,' Mr

Bunting said to his ashen-faced wife.

'Hmm,' she said, looking nervously about her. She had spotted, to her horror, that the pictures in the hall, which had been hanging perfectly straight on their arrival, were now all wonky.

Sparky had been busy. 'Erm, do we really need to go upstairs?' she said. 'I think we're after something a little more modern, aren't we, darling?' She looked pleadingly at her husband.

Unfortunately for her, Mr Bunting, always with an eye for a bargain, was beginning to wonder how much he could knock the price down in the light of all the problems the house seemed to have.

'Oh, I think we should see the whole place now we're here,' he said.

Unwillingly, Mrs Bunting followed them up the staircase.

'In addition to this floor, there are also some extremely spacious attic rooms,' Clive went on.

Right on cue, Archie flicked a switch on the sound system.

Thump! Thump! Thump!

Loud noises came from the attic.

Mr Bunting paused, wide-eyed, becoming a little less keen. Clive was beginning to look panic stricken but bravely soldiered on.

'Flo,' said Archie through their communication system, 'you take it from here.'

Clive had turned towards the stairs, his back to the landing. He looked at Mr and Mrs Bunting, and watched the remaining colour drain from their faces as their eyes moved from side to side, as if they were watching something.

They were.

Behind Clive, Flo was hidden underneath a large white sheet and was gliding backwards and forwards across the landing. Her eyes glowed green beneath the sheet for maximum effect.

Without a word, Mr Bunting pointed open-mouthed at the apparition.

Clive swallowed hard. He knew that the expressions on their faces were unlikely to be the result of noticing the house's stunning original features. It was very likely something quite different, something he really didn't want to see himself. Reluctantly, he turned around.

'AAAAAAARRGGH!' he yelled on behalf of all of them and they all ran. There was a scramble down the stairs for the door. Clive won.

In less than a minute, they'd disappeared in a cloud of dust as the estate agent's car sped off down the driveway.

When they had finally stopped laughing, the Petbots sat at the top of the stairs, very pleased with themselves.

'That was SO easy!' Archie said.

'Much easier than I expected,' said Flo.

Sparky was so excited he was spinning around in circles all over the landing. 'I want to do it again!' he squeaked.

'If everyone is that easy to scare,' said Archie, 'the place will be ours forever. Who'd want to live in a haunted house?'

Chapter 4

Terrible Tuesday

For the next few of weeks, things became pretty routine. Clive would turn up with a prospective buyer – the other estate agents at his branch had refused to go anywhere near the place after his spooky stories – and the Petbots would scare them off. Clive himself almost became used to it all in the end, but he still hated going.

As time went on and word got around, the number of visits dwindled and the Petbots began to feel quite safe.

One fateful Tuesday though, everything changed.

'Clive's on his way!' called Flo. She flew down from the chimney and joined the others who were soaking up solar rays in the garden.

'Thanks, Flo,' said Archie. 'Switching to internal communications. Positions, everyone!' He dashed down to the basement and sat at the control panel. 'They're just coming in, Sparky.'

'Okay, I'm ready,' said Sparky, poised for action in the kitchen.

Clive opened the door. 'The first time I came here, Mr Dawkins, I thought I was going crazy – you know, overworked or something,' Clive was explaining to an eager-looking man. The buyer was round and bald, and wore a plain brown suit, but his waistcoat was the most colourful thing Archie had ever seen.

'So you say, so you say.' The man squealed as though he was about to burst with excitement. 'It sounds ideal! I want you to show me everything.'

'I usually start my tour in the kitchen.'

'Lead on, lead on.' Mr Dawkins seemed to enjoy saying everything twice.

'As I have explained . . .' sighed Clive, entering the kitchen and knowing exactly what was about to happen.

Clatter!
Crash!

Sparky knocked down a couple of pans, as usual.

Clive didn't take much notice. He was so used to it now, he just looked a little queasy.

However, Mr Dawkins, despite his roundness, jumped a metre into the air. But strangely he seemed more fascinated than afraid.

'Then there's the basement,' Clive continued, pointing towards it.

Right on cue, the door slammed shut.

But instead of being scared, Mr Dawkins clapped his hands.

'This is not good,' said Archie. He was beginning to get a bad feeling about this particular house-hunter.

'What's next on the tour?' asked Mr Dawkins.

Clive turned and the basement door swung open again.

'Lovely, lovely, just as you described!' said Mr Dawkins.

Back in the hall, Sparky was ready to do his next job.

'Step it up a bit, Sparky,' said Archie over their communications. 'This guy doesn't scare easily. Flo, when it's time for your performance, give it all you've got.'

Sparky not only made the pictures wonky, he used his laser eyes to cut their strings so they dropped and rattled on the floor.

'That's new,' said Clive. 'They've never fallen down before.'

'Fantastic! Fantastic!' Mr Dawkins was thrilled.

Archie was puzzled. He turned up the volume on the sound system.

Thump! Thump! Thump!

48

The noises echoed round the big old house.

THUMP! THUMP! THUMP!

'The last thing we see is the ghost itself,' whispered Clive.

'Wooo! WOOOOOOO!' boomed Archie as Flo

burst onto the landing and swept downstairs, her eyes glowing bright green under the sheet.

'Amazing!' whispered Mr Dawkins, awestruck.

Clive backed away from the stairs. 'I'll wait outside,' he said. 'Let me know when you're ready to go.'

'Indeed, indeed,' said Mr Dawkins. He took a mobile phone from his pocket and made a call,

while Flo continued to circle above him and Archie broadcast sounds of mournful moaning, chain rattling and the odd piercing scream over the hidden speakers.

'Hello, Clara, it's me. It's all true! I'm standing here in the presence of a real apparition. It's absolutely fantastic. I can't believe after all these years I've finally found it. This will be the perfect place for the world's first ever genuine haunted house hotel. I'm going straight back to the estate agent's to sign on the dotted line.' There was a pause while the person on the other end of the line spoke to Mr Dawkins. 'Yes, I know, Clara, it's great news. I can't wait to get the builders in.'

Flo swooped down low enough to stare him straight in the eyes.

'Tremendous! Tremendous!' he shrieked. 'Have to go, Clara, speak to you later.' He pocketed his phone and ran to the front door. 'Clive! Clive!' he said. 'I'll take it!'

When he'd gone, the Petbots sat dejectedly at the bottom of the stairs.

'Looks like we'll be moving after all,' said Archie.

'But I don't want to move. This is our home,' said Flo. 'All our memories are here.'

'We've no choice,' said Archie. 'Not now. How were we to know ghosts were what he was looking for?'

'I suppose we'd better start packing. There's a lot to do,' said Flo.

'Let's start tomorrow,' said Archie. 'I can't face doing anything now.'

'Me neither,' sighed Sparky. 'Anyway, I don't know about you two, but I'm worn out! I need a recharge.'

Flo nodded. They wandered slowly into the garden and sat in the sun to charge their batteries.

Archie knew they were going to be leaving the only home they'd ever had. The house was full of their memories of the Professor and it would be like losing him all over again.

'Where will we go?' asked Flo. 'Who will take care of us?'

'We'll have to look after each other from now on, Flo,' answered Archie. 'Don't worry, we'll be okay. The Professor taught us well.'

Sparky wheeled over closer to the others. 'We're a good team, aren't we?' he said nervously.

'Good?' said Archie. 'We're a *great* team. And we've always got each other – that's what counts.'

Chapter 5

In Hiding

The next morning, the Petbots were woken by a terrible racket outside. They rushed to the attic window to see what was going on. Mr Dawkins was standing in the driveway, talking on his mobile. Archie picked up the conversation and played it through his speakers.

'Yes, I know it's quick, but I paid cash and

signed the papers last night. I want the place locked up securely by lunchtime. Everything is to be strictly hush-hush until the grand opening. The house clearance team will be here on Friday so that the builders can start working on the place first thing Monday. I'm going to take some photos, then I'm off to meet with the architect.'

'Oh no!' shrieked Flo, horrified.

'I know, it doesn't give us long, does it?' replied Archie.

'It's Wednesday already,' said Sparky.

'Okay, here's what we do,' said Archie. He looked very serious. 'We'll seal up this room, to keep our stuff safe, then get down to the basement and lock ourselves in, so we won't be found if Dawkins starts poking around.'

'Guys, that's not our only problem,' said Flo. 'Look!'

All around the house and garden a high fence was being erected with barbed wire on the top. Not only that, but a man wearing a bright yellow hard hat and carrying a matching toolbox was

putting up little signs that said, *Danger: Electrified Fence.*

'Oh no!' said Archie. 'It gets worse. That will fry our circuits if we touch it!'

They heard the front door open.

'Quick! Basement!' said Archie.

'They'll see you!' said Sparky. 'Get under the sheet,' said Flo. 'I can hide you.' They locked the attic door behind them and set off,

just as Mr Dawkins came into the hall. He clapped his hands in delight when he saw the trail of white drift past and down into the basement. Once inside, Archie slammed the door shut and activated the electromagnetic lock.

'What now?' said Flo.

'Now,' said Archie, 'we watch the video diaries again and make a list of everything we need to pack. Then, when everybody has gone, we can get what we need from upstairs.'

'That's all very well but what about the electrified fence? How will you get through it?' asked Flo. 'It's okay for me, I can fly over it and I could probably carry Sparky. But what about you, Archie? And what about all the stuff we need to take?'

'I'll think of something,' said Archie, desperately

trying to think of something.

Flo and Sparky looked at each other nervously.

'Don't worry,' said Archie. 'Like the Professor used to say, *There's always a solution – we just need to find it.*'

They settled down to watch the Professor's farewell film once more and Archie created a list of everything they would need to take, then printed it out and stuck it up on the wall. The list was very long.

For the rest of the day, the Petbots kept themselves busy assembling all the items on the list that were kept in the basement. They packed boxes of bolts, nuts, screws and wires. They collected cartons of cogs, printed circuits, cameras and cables. They gathered computer software and hardware, books, plans . . . It all made quite a pile.

When at last everything was quiet upstairs and it was clear they had the place to themselves again, they emerged from the basement.

'Flo,' said Archie, 'can you get together the things you want to take from the rest of the house? Just remember we won't have a lot of room.'

'Okay!' said Flo, and flapped off happily.

'Sparky.'

'Yes, boss!' said Sparky, raring to go.

'Zip around and see if you can find anything that we can use as a trailer.'

He whizzed off in a spray of sparks.

Archie headed to the study to collect the rest of the Professor's notebooks. He passed the living room, where the Professor and the Petbots had spent happy evenings together watching his favourite DVDs. They had done that more in recent times as the Professor had got older and less active. Archie felt sad. He missed the Professor and their chats about this and that, and he missed them all watching the DVDs together.

'Maybe we should take a few with us!' he thought.

He wandered over to take a look. There wasn't a huge collection and a lot of them were about inventors. There were some really old films like *Frankenstein*, *20,000 Leagues Under the Sea*, *The Time Machine* and . . .'That's it!' exclaimed Archie.

'*The Great Escape*! The Prof's absolute favourite. Flo! FLO! I've got it!' he yelled. He sounded so excited that both Flo and Sparky came to see what was going on. He was waving *The Great Escape* DVD in the air excitedly.

'A tunnel!' said Archie. 'That's how we'll get out – we'll dig a tunnel, just like they do in this movie!'

Flo didn't seem convinced. 'How?' she asked.

'Once, when we'd watched the film, I asked the Professor how he would have done it – tunnelled out from a prison, I mean,' explained Archie. 'He showed me sketches of a tunnelling machine he'd designed to show how easy it could be. They were on the computer, I'm sure. I'd better get started.'

'Let me get this straight,' said Flo. 'You're going to build a tunnelling machine to get us out of here.'

'Got it in one!' said Archie.

'Isn't that a little ambitious?' she said.

'Do you have any better ideas?'

Flo didn't.

'We still need a trailer, though,' said Sparky. 'I haven't found anything like that yet.'

Archie stared absent-mindedly at the DVD cover of a man on a motorbike.

'Hang on,' he said, 'didn't the Professor have a motorbike?'

'Oh yes, I remember!' Flo said dreamily. 'He used to take us for drives in – the sidecar! Of course! That would be perfect.'

'Is it still in the garage?'

'It could be the big lump under the tarpaulin covered with cobwebs and dust,' said Sparky.

They dashed out to the garage, pulled off the tarpaulin and there it was.

'Bingo!' said Archie.

They uncoupled the sidecar and between them managed to pull, push and squeeze it down the stairs to the basement.

'Right!' said Archie. 'I'd better get a move on. I've got a tunnelling machine to build.'

'I want to help,' said Sparky.

'Me too,' agreed Flo.

'There's not much you can do right now, I'll

need to really concentrate on what I'm doing to get it right.'

They looked disappointed.

'But there's a whole lot of stuff I need to get together before I start. The list will be on the computer. It will save some time if you can get it all organised for me.'

'Okay,' said Sparky and Flo together, happy to be able to do something useful.

'But after that you should get some rest. I'll need you fresh and fully charged first thing in the morning.'

They went down to the basement and Archie gave them the list. They were off in a flash.

Then Archie stared at the workshop filled with diagrams, mountains of metal, tons of tools and reels of wire. It wasn't going to be easy.

'Oh dear,' he sighed. 'Where on earth do I start?'

Chapter 6

Digging For Victory

Archie worked all night. With the Professor's plans to follow, it wasn't too difficult – well, not for Archie who loved building things, and the Professor had trained him well. But there was still a lot to do. He'd kept his charge up by staying plugged into the mains so he could work at full speed.

When Flo and Sparky came down from the attic first thing in the morning, Archie was putting the finishing touches to the machine.

'Have you been charging on full power all night?' asked Flo. 'You know that's not good for you. You'll burn out your circuits.'

'I had no choice,' said Archie, 'we don't have much time.'

'Well, you don't need it now,' she said, unplugging his charging lead. 'It looks finished.'

'Almost,' said Archie. 'Soon we can try it out.'

'I hope it's not too noisy,' said Flo. 'Someone might come down here and investigate.'

'Yeah, I thought of that,' said Archie. 'I looped some more ghostly sound effects and set them up to play automatically through the sound system. If they are loud enough while the tunnel gets started, it should be okay. Once the digger goes underground there shouldn't be a problem.'

'Cool!' said Flo.

Sparky was zipping round and round the new machine. 'Can we try it out?' he squeaked. 'It looks awesome!'

'We have to make a hole in the concrete floor first,' Archie told him.

'Flo and I can do that with the Prof's big drill,' said Sparky. 'Come on, Flo.'

They dragged the pneumatic drill over to a likely spot for the tunnel entrance and got to work. Before long they'd made a hole big enough for the machine to start drilling into the earth.

'Just in time,' said Flo. 'Sounds like the workmen have arrived.'

She was right. Outside, several rubbish skips were being delivered, ready for the major work planned for the old house.

'I hope we're gone before they start,' said Flo mournfully. 'It would be horrible to see them tearing up our home.'

'If this works the way it should,' said Archie, 'we'll be gone faster than an electric current!' Despite his confident words, Archie was rather nervous that the tunnelling machine might not work. He'd never built something so big without the Professor before, and he'd had to replace some of the parts in the original design with others he'd had to adapt himself. He was worried about the motor too. He'd used the one off the old motorbike but had no idea how long it would last. 'I've made some measurements, and this shows how far we need to go to clear the fence,' Archie said, pointing to a plan he'd drawn. 'I've installed a sensor and a camera at the front so that we can take readings of how far it's got.'

'So, is it ready to go?' asked Sparky.

'Yep,' said Archie. 'Paws crossed. Flo, turn on the sound effects for our unwelcome visitors.'

A cacophony of banging, clanking and wailing rang out from the speakers upstairs.

'That should do the trick,' she giggled.

'Okay! Here we go!' said Archie, and flicked the digger's *On* switch.

The tunnelling machine burst into life, quickly spraying them with little bits of mud and stone.

'Ow!' said Archie. 'I think I'd better reduce power a bit.' He turned a control dial and the machine slowed to a steadier pace.

'It's working!' said Flo. 'Well done, Archie.' She wrapped her wings around him and hugged him tight.

'Never doubted it for a moment!' he lied.

'Er, there is one thing,' Sparky said. 'What are we going to do with the earth that comes out of the hole?'

'That bendy hose will feed it into the store room at the back of the basement,' said Archie.

'You've thought of everything.' Flo was clearly impressed.

Archie, deservedly, looked quite smug.

From upstairs all that could be heard was a low, humming sound from the basement and loud, scary sounds from the rest of the house. They could even be heard from outside. The lorry driver delivering the skips was terrified.

'I'm not hanging around here any longer than I have to,' he said to himself as he sped off down the driveway. He made a mental note not to be available when the skips needed collecting.

He was the lucky one. Standing on the front doorstep, shaking like a leaf at the sounds coming out from the house, was the petrified architect.

Standing with him was Mr Dawkins, who was talking animatedly about his plans.

'. . . and on the third floor – the attic, as it is now – I think we can squeeze in another four rooms. You should come in and take a look around.'

'NO!' shouted the architect. 'Just give me the original floor plans and a list of the alterations you want,' he said as he backed away. He was

already nearly halfway down the driveway. 'Come and see me in the office in a couple of days.' He turned and ran shouting back over his shoulder. 'Bye!' And he was gone.

Mr Dawkins went inside.

'Fabulous!' he chuckled. 'Even more noise than before. The ghosts are clearly resenting our presence.' He went upstairs with his camera talking to himself all the time, and all the time Archie listened. 'Right. Photos and plans for the top two floors today. Tomorrow I'll do the ground floor and then, when the house clearers come, I'll get that basement door broken down.'

Archie looked at the others. The race to dig was on – Dawkins was closing in.

Chapter 7

Tunnel Trouble

Down in the basement, the Petbots were packing. They were putting everything they needed in the small luggage compartment at the back of the sidecar.

'We need to travel at night to make sure no one sees us, but we can squeeze into the sidecar during the day or if we have to hide for any reason,' said Archie.

'How will we charge our batteries if we're in the dark all day?' asked Flo.

'Good point,' replied Archie. 'We'd better put some solar panels on the outside and we can plug ourselves into them.'

'Is everything going to fit?' asked Sparky.

'Pretty much,' said Archie. 'I'm not sure we need to take the houseplant though, Flo.'

Flo looked upset. She was finding the idea of moving very stressful.

'Well, perhaps, you could just take part of it, rather than the whole thing,' Archie suggested.

'I suppose so,' she said, and started to examine the plant for a suitable bit to put in a smaller pot.

'Where do you think we're going to end up?' asked Sparky.

'I'm not sure,' said Archie. He was putting on a brave face but he was really quite worried. He had no experience of being outside in the 'real' world, and no idea where they should head. 'Let's see how far we've tunnelled!' he said, trying to change the subject. He went over to the computer and switched on the camera attached to the front of the tunnelling machine.

'What an exciting view!' Flo said. 'Mud.'

'It's gone fifteen metres – eighty-five more to go.

It's going to be a close call. The house clearance team arrive tomorrow.'

There was nothing they could do but wait. They watched on the CCTV as Dawkins pottered about

happily, packing boxes for the house clearance team. Then they watched the tunnel as it moved forward bit by bit. By lunchtime it had reached forty-five metres and the Petbots were beginning to feel quite hopeful.

'You know,' said Flo, 'I just had a thought. Mr Dawkins is going to be rather disappointed.'

'How do you mean?' asked Archie.

'Think about it. When we go, so do the "ghosts". It won't be much of a *haunted* hotel.'

They looked at each other and burst out laughing.

'Oh dear,' chuckled Sparky. 'What about his grand opening?'

'Poor man!' snorted Archie. 'I almost feel sorry for him now.'

'I think it will be hysterical. Serves him right for being greedy and making us homeless,' said Flo.

By the time it was quiet again upstairs, the machine had only tunnelled another ten metres. It had been tough. Archie had spent the day steering the machine round various obstacles. There were tree roots, rocks, sewage pipes – even a couple of rabbit warrens containing some very worried-looking rabbits.

'It's just over halfway. We're not going to make it, are we? What's going to happen if it's not finished before the workmen come?' said Flo.

'I don't know,' said Archie. He was worried too.

'We can leave it on all night though, can't we?' asked Flo.

'We'll have to,' said Archie. 'Hey, I can leave it on autopilot for a bit. Let's go upstairs – it might be our last chance to say goodbye to the old place.'

They emerged from the basement to see that the hallway was filled with boxes packed with the contents of the house. There were two piles. One pile said *Rubbish* the other said *Store*.

'Dawkins has been busy,' Archie observed.

They looked inside the boxes.

'At least he's keeping some of the Professor's stuff for the hotel. I guess he wants to keep it authentic. What's in the rubbish pile, Flo?'

'Clothes and stuff mostly,' sniffed Flo, as she pulled out one of the Professor's long woolly scarves. She'd made it herself for his last birthday. 'Is there room in the sidecar for this?' she asked.

Archie looked at her sad face and didn't have the heart to say no.

'Sure,' he said. 'We can squeeze it in.'

They all trundled up the stairs for a last look at the attic. It was completely empty.

'Doesn't feel much like home any more, does it?' said Sparky, zipping back and forth across the floor. The evening sun shone through the attic window and lit up the puffs of dust Sparky's wheels sent into the air.

'Let's go and sit in the garden for a bit,' sighed Archie.

They sat outside and soaked up the last rays of the sun, reminiscing about the old days.

Archie began to laugh.

'Do you remember when the wind-powered lawnmower went crazy?'

'Oh yes,' said Flo. 'It was hilarious.'

'Until it wrecked my vegetable patch,' Sparky said, wincing.

'And chased Archie round and round the garden!' giggled Flo.

'It would have trampled me too, if the Prof hadn't caught it in time,' said Sparky.

'And he ended up in the fish pond, but couldn't climb out because he couldn't stop laughing!' Flo smiled.

'Good times!' said Archie.

They watched the first stars appear in the sky and listened to the gentle hum of the tunnelling machine beneath them.

'Our last day,' thought Archie. 'I shall really miss this place.'

They went back to the basement to check the progress of the tunnel.

'Seventy-five metres,' said Sparky brightly. 'Not too far now.'

'Hmm, we have to hope we don't hit any rocky patches,' said Archie. 'As soon as it's reached its target we have to dig upwards to get to the surface. But that should only be a metre or so.'

Suddenly an alarm sounded on the tunnelling machine. Archie ran over to see what the problem was.

'Clay!' said Archie. 'I hoped this wouldn't happen. It's much harder to dig through and it's overheating the machine. I'll have to reduce the power for a while.' He frowned. 'It's going to slow us down.'

By ten o'clock the tunnel had only gone a few metres further, and at midnight disaster struck.

BANG!

A plume of black smoke billowed out from the tunnel and filled the basement.

'That's it,' said Archie, frowning. 'The motor's blown. How far has it got, Sparky?'

Sparky checked the monitor. 'Eighty-nine metres,' he said.

'Is that enough?' asked Flo.

'It will have to be,' said Archie. 'Okay!' he added in a positive voice, 'let's push the sidecar into the tunnel. It's time to go.'

Chapter 8

Freedom

The Petbots made their way along the tunnel, with Archie pulling the sidecar like a carthorse. He'd rigged up a harness that clipped onto the front of the sidecar, but dragging it along was hard work on the bumpy earth floor of the tunnel. Despite his robot strength, Archie could only move slowly. But worse, the effort put such a strain on his batteries that the torch beams from his eyes, which lit the way ahead, were already beginning to dim.

'Phew!' he said. 'This is tough.'

Flo suddenly had a disturbing thought. 'Archie,' she asked as calmly as she could manage, 'what if the tunnel collapses while we're in it?'

Archie had been hoping that no one would ask him that.

He was worried that the digger's motor blowing up the way it did might have weakened the tunnel. For all Archie knew, it could collapse at any time. The slower they went, the longer they'd be in the tunnel – and every moment that they spent in the tunnel was a risk.

This wasn't something Archie chose to share with the others.

'Then we dig our way out of it, of course,' he

replied confidently. 'It's not like we're going to suffocate. Stop worrying.'

This was true, of course, but Archie knew the real danger was that if they were buried, they'd run out of energy. They were solar-powered, and there would be no light to charge their batteries. They could be stuck there forever! Either that or they'd be crushed like tin cans. He shivered.

There was a rumbling sound behind Flo. Little bits of mud and small stones dropped onto the top of the sidecar, and she began to wish she had chosen to fly over the fence and meet them outside. Flo had made the decision to join them in the tunnel in case her help was needed. Now she was wondering how wise that was. 'Then again,' she thought, 'I couldn't have let them do this alone.'

'OW!' yelped Sparky, and dashed for cover under the sidecar after a larger stone hit him on the nose.

The rumbling got a little louder and, without a word to each other, they all started moving faster.

'I can see the digger just up ahead,' said Archie, relieved. 'Not far now.'

When they reached the machine, it was still smoking gently.

'Right,' said Archie, 'onwards and upwards.' He removed one of the hole-tunnelling tools from the side of the digger and attached a round handle. He and Flo each grabbed on, pointed it to the roof of the tunnel and started to turn.

At the other end of the tunnel the rumbling was even louder now, and larger bits of mud and stone began to crumble away from the ceiling. From the corner of his eye, Archie spotted a crack in the tunnel roof appear near the machine. The Petbots looked nervously at each other.

Quickly, Sparky wrapped his tail around the handle and engaged his turbo boost. He only ever used it in a dire emergency and it would only last for a minute or two, but this was just the sort of

emergency he imagined the Professor had designed it for. Instantly the borer turned twice as fast. Once they got a rhythm going, it turned faster and faster until . . .

'Stop!' shouted Archie. A little shaft of moonlight shone through a small hole above them. 'We're through!'

He climbed on top of the sidecar to widen the hole, extend his neck and poke his head out to take a look.

'It's the surface,' he called down. 'We've made it!'

As quickly as he could, Archie unpacked ramps

and placed them in front of sidecar wheels. Meanwhile, Sparky and Flo clamped a hook with a thick rope to the front of the sidecar.

'Okay,' he said, 'when I say "Go", push for all you're worth!'

Flo and Sparky nodded.

Archie took out the other end of the rope and quickly attached the hook to himself. He climbed up out of the hole. It was good to feel the cool night air after being in the hot, stuffy tunnel.

He emerged on the other side of the electric fence, in a patch of waste ground opposite the house. There was no one anywhere to be seen. Archie wrapped the rope around his body and prepared himself.

'GO!' called Archie, and pulled with all his strength. It was hard. He extended his metal claws into the earth for a better grip and pulled even harder.

Back in the tunnel, Flo and Sparky pushed with all their might.

'I wish I had some turbo left!' groaned Sparky. Sparks flew off his wheels as he pushed as hard as he could.

'I wish you did too!' said Flo, straining with the effort.

The sidecar shifted onto the ramp with a jolt and began to advance slowly towards the surface.

'Phew!' said Flo. 'It's finally moving.'

But her relief was short-lived. The loudest rumble they'd heard so far shook the tunnel. Flo

turned to look behind her and switched on her night vision. A landslide of earth was heading right towards them – fast! 'Push harder, Sparky!' she shouted.

Archie could even hear the rumble from outside, and knew the tunnel was finally giving way. He gritted his teeth and pulled until he thought his cogs would burst. Then, at last, the sidecar suddenly popped out of the hole, and

Archie ran to tie the harness to a nearby pole to stop it from sliding back.

He called to Flo and Sparky as he raced to the hole. 'Quick!' he said. 'You've got to get out of there! The tunnel is about to —'

CRASH!

The tunnel exit crumbled into a pile of dirt and stone.

'Flo! Sparky!' cried Archie. 'Oh NO!'

He ran over and frantically began to dig with his paws, all the time calling their names in desperation.

Suddenly he saw a glint of metal in the moonlight. It was Flo's beak!

'Flo! Flo! Are you all right? Where's Sparky?' asked Archie as he dug around to free her.

She emerged spluttering, spitting out bits of

dirt and gravel, and there, tucked tightly under one wing, was Sparky.

'Thank goodness!' sighed Archie.

The three of them collapsed in a heap on the ground next to the ruined tunnel.

'We can't go back now,' said Archie, 'even if we wanted to.'

When the Petbots had dusted themselves off and recovered a bit, they looked around. It was the very first time they'd been out of the house on their own, apart from when Flo had occasionally flown to the post box on the corner of their road to send a letter for the Professor.

'It's scary,' said Sparky.

'It's exciting too,' said Archie. 'Come on, we'd better get moving.'

He put the rope in the sidecar, attached himself to the harness, and they were ready to go.

'Which way?' said Flo.

'Let's go, um, that way,' said Archie, pointing to the flattest route he could see. He didn't really fancy the idea of having to pull the sidecar uphill.

They set off enthusiastically, wondering what their next home would be like. Secretly they all hoped to find somewhere just like the Professor's house but they knew deep down that wasn't going to happen.

They travelled all night, passing not even a single building. By the time the stars began to fade, they had covered quite a distance and they seemed to have reached some sort of industrial area.

'It's nearly daylight,' said Archie. 'We'd better find somewhere to hide.'

Flo stretched her wings. 'I'll take a look up ahead,' she said.

Archie could feel his battery draining. 'I really need a rest,' he said to Sparky, who was slowing down as well.

Within a minute Flo was back.

'Just around the next bend,' she said, 'there's a scrapyard with a hole in its fence. It's not big enough for the sidecar, but we can make it bigger.'

'Perfect. Where better to hide a bunch of old metal than in a scrapyard full of it?' Archie smiled, but his eyes began to dim and flicker.

'Your battery must almost be out. Do you think

you can make it?' Flo was worried. She was feeling drained herself.

'I should be okay,' replied Archie bravely. 'I can see the scrapyard just ahead.'

Flo and Sparky did their best to ease the load by pulling it along with him and, thankfully, after a few minutes they reached the hole in the fence. Flo set to work with her powerful beak and snipped through the metal chain link. They pushed the edges back as far as they could and, with a couple of minor scrapes, the sidecar popped through.

Archie had just enough energy left to pull the sidecar over to what they hoped was a quiet corner of the scrapyard. They rolled a couple of old tyres in front of it for camouflage, crawled into the luggage compartment, plugged into the solar chargers and settled down to rest just as dawn broke above them.

The scrapyard was a very noisy place. As the Petbots lay charging their batteries later that morning, all they could hear was the banging and crashing of old cars being picked up and crushed in the compactor. Sparky was sitting on top of the sidecar watching. He found it fascinating. A huge round electromagnet dangled off the end of a crane. It swung round

to pick up the cars and drop them into a crusher, which turned them into big cubes of metal.

'Fifteen!' he squeaked. 'That's fifteen cubes of metal it's made this morning!'

The crane moved off to a different part of the yard further away and out of sight.

'Oh!' moaned Sparky in disappointment. 'I was enjoying that.'

He settled back into the sidecar and the

Petbots discussed what their next move should be.

'Maybe we could stay here,' suggested Sparky. 'We're tucked away in the corner – no one would notice us. And there'd be loads of useful spare parts in the scrapyard.'

But Flo didn't like the idea at all. 'What if we got turned into scrap?!' she said. 'Besides, I don't like it here, it's too noisy.'

'It's not ideal,' said Archie, 'but it may be okay for now, Flo.'

'I suppose so,' she reluctantly agreed.

'We wouldn't be able to wander around during the day though,' continued Archie. 'Well, Sparky could – he's small enough not to be noticed – but we will need to move on and find somewhere more permanent eventually.'

'What's that noise?' asked Flo.

'Which noise?' said Archie. 'The crane or the crusher?'

'No, that humming sound,' she said. 'The one that's getting louder.'

Huummmm m m m.

'Oh yes, I can hear it now,' said Sparky. 'It's coming from —'

Suddenly, Sparky flew from one side of the sidecar to the other and stuck fast to the top.

The Petbots all looked at each other.

'ELECTROMAGNET!' they said in unison.

Archie and Flo poked their heads outside. Sure
enough, the crane was coming towards them and
was picking up little bits and pieces of metal like a
giant vacuum cleaner.

They felt the sidecar wobble a bit.

'Oh no! I told you!' yelled Flo. 'We're going to
be scrapped!'

She watched with wide eyes as pieces of metal about the size of her and Sparky were pulled towards the giant magnet. They hit it with a metallic ping.

'Stay inside, whatever you do!' said Archie. 'Everything out there the size of you two is going to end up on that magnet.' Archie grabbed the rope they'd used to get the sidecar out of the tunnel. He hooked one end of it to the underneath of the sidecar. 'Wish me luck!' he said, and he took the other end and headed for the fence.

'Archie, no!' Flo was in a real panic.

'It's okay, Flo,' Archie called, 'I'm bigger and heavier than you. I'll be all right.' He darted between the flying chunks of scrap, hoping that no one would notice there was a robot cat in the scrapyard, tearing towards the fence like a maniac.

He reached it just in time. As Archie hooked the rope around one of the fence posts, the electromagnet swung past the sidecar, picking up stray hubcaps, wheels and other pieces of metal debris as it did.

Inside the sidecar, Flo
hung on tightly. The
sidecar rattled and shook
and strained against the
rope. Anything that was
metal and not screwed
down shot to one side of

the sidecar, where Sparky was squeaking in alarm.

Outside, Archie held on tightly to the rope, just
to be sure, and shut his eyes. He imagined for a
moment what would have happened if Sparky had
been outside the sidecar when the electromagnet
had swung past, and then he pushed the thought
from his mind.

The sidecar wobbled and pulled against the
rope, but thanks to the hook, and Archie's

strength, the sidecar was saved from the crusher.

After what seemed like a lifetime, but was only really a minute or two, the sound of humming grew fainter. The rope began to slacken and Archie opened his eyes.

'Phew!' he said.

Archie could see Flo's anxious face peeking out to see if he was okay. He darted back across the yard to his friends.

Sparky crawled out, looking a bit dazed and wobbly.

'I've changed my mind,' he said. 'I don't want to live here after all.'

Chapter 9

Homeless

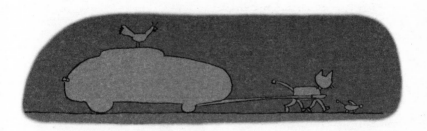

As soon as it was night, the Petbots left the scrapyard and continued their search for a new home. It was very dark – the moon was hidden by thick, gloomy-looking clouds.

'Looks like rain's coming,' said Flo.

'That's all we need,' groaned Archie. 'Rain and robots don't exactly mix very well.'

'I'll fly ahead,' Flo said. 'Not far enough to run my batteries down, but I might see something useful.'

She flew above some houses and landed on a chimney to survey the world around them. She

switched on her night vision so that she could see better, but it still didn't look hopeful. They seemed to be on the outskirts of a town and the few buildings she could see looked like they were occupied. She noticed there was a railway line. 'Maybe we should follow that,' she thought. 'It should take us nearer town. There might be more people around but there would probably be more places to hide.' She felt a few spots of rain run down her feathers. 'Or just to shelter from the rain!'

By the time Flo got back to Archie, Sparky and the sidecar, it was raining quite heavily.

'It's no good,' said Archie, 'we have to get under cover and out of this rain.'

'There are some railway arches just around the next corner. We can shelter there until it stops raining,' said Flo.

'Great. You and Sparky go on ahead while I pull the sidecar,' Archie said. 'No point in all of us getting soaked.'

It seemed like ages to Flo and Sparky before Archie made it to the railway arch, and when he did, he was completely drenched.

'At least it's dry under here,' said Flo as she helped him take off the harness.

Archie stood dripping, creating a little puddle on the dry ground. 'I feel like I'm seizing up already. Hope I don't go rusty.'

'We just need to get you dry.' Flo remembered how the Professor used to dry off by the living room fire after a walk in the rain, and she had an idea. 'Sparky, help me find some dry stuff and we can build a fire.'

There was plenty of suitable rubbish under the arch to make a fire – old newspapers, twigs, cardboard boxes – even a broken wooden pallet. Flo and Sparky gathered it all together into a pile, then Sparky whizzed round and round creating sparks that jumped onto the rubbish pile. Once they smouldered, Flo flapped her wings to blow air onto the sparks, to help the fire catch hold. Once the fire was going, they all felt a little happier, although Sparky was feeling rather dizzy.

'We may as well stay here for a bit,' said Archie. 'It might be dark and dingy but it's obviously uninhabited. Maybe we could make something of it, give it a door, perhaps. It might work.'

Flo shuffled closer to the fire. 'It's a bit dirty and smelly.'

'It's better than nothing, though,' said Sparky. 'And no electromagnets,' he added with a shiver.

They stared at the flames until they began to die away, then curled up together and settled down to rest.

They were awoken at dawn by the most incredible noise rumbling through the walls. It was the

loudest thing they'd ever heard in their lives.

'Help!' screamed Flo. 'It's an earthquake!'

Sparky was visibly shaking.

'It's a train!' yelled Archie. 'Had you forgotten we're under a railway arch? There'll probably be another one along in a minute or so.'

Sure enough, as Archie predicted, a few minutes later . . .

RUMBLE! RUMBLE! RUMBLE!

'This is awful!' said Flo. 'My circuits are all shaken up!'

Every twenty minutes or so from then on, two trains went over the railway arch.

'Clearly,' said Archie, trying to cover his ears, 'this isn't going to work. We'd be deaf in a week.'

'I wish the sidecar was soundproof,' winced Flo as another train rumbled by. 'We're going to be stuck here until dark.'

'You two could go and find somewhere quieter,' said Archie. 'I'll stay here.'

'No,' said Flo. She still felt bad for leaving Archie alone in the rain the night before. 'We should stick together. Hey, I've got an idea!'

Flo disappeared into the sidecar. She emerged a few minutes later with a long scarf.

'You brought a scarf?' said Sparky, puzzled. 'Are you cold?'

'No, silly,' said Flo, 'it's the Professor's favourite.' She flew over and wound it around Archie's ears.

'Ah!' he said. 'Clever Flo!'

Then she wrapped it around herself and Sparky.

'It should help block out the noise a bit,' she said.

So there they sat, watching the rain and listening to the trains rumble overhead.

'I hope we have more luck tonight,' moaned Sparky. He looked dejectedly at his fellow Petbots.

'Don't we all?' agreed Archie.

Eventually, the trains stopped running and the rain stopped raining. The Petbots set off on their third night of searching for a new home. They were getting desperate. Being homeless was no fun at all and more than ever they realised how happy they'd been living with the Professor.

'At least there are more buildings around here,' said Sparky.

'Yes,' agreed Archie, 'but none of them are empty.'

'Shall I scout ahead again?' asked Flo.

'You may as well,' said Archie. They watched her fly away. 'I'm definitely feeling a bit stiff today, Sparky, how about you?'

'I'm okay,' said Sparky, 'but I wasn't in the rain as long as you.'

'I think I'm developing a rusty squeak,' complained Archie.

They trudged on miserably.

Meanwhile, Flo, who was about a mile or so away, found herself flying over a shopping mall. She could see the train station up ahead and was about to turn back when something caught her eye.

'It's just like home!' she exclaimed. Quite near the station, on the edge of town, was a building

that reminded her of the Professor's house, but bigger. The best thing was that it had an attic room just like their own. 'I don't believe it,' she said. She flew over to get a better look.

Flo did a circuit of the building, looking in every window. No one was inside. There was a high wall around the property, with a locked gate. There were no cars parked anywhere, and when she perched on the window ledge of the attic and looked inside it was obvious that no one had been up there for years. There were a few boxes but everything was covered in thick layers of dust and cobwebs.

'Fantastic!' Flo said to herself. 'It's perfect!' She couldn't wait to tell the others. Off she flew, wings flapping as fast as she could manage.

Archie and Sparky spotted Flo in the distance, coming towards them at full speed. They could tell she was excited.

'I've found it! I've found it!' she shrieked. She landed on the sidecar and flapped her wings excitedly. 'It's wonderful! It's just like home, and there's no one there!'

'How far is it, Flo?' asked Archie, hoping that their quest was over.

'Not far at all. It shouldn't take more than half an hour. We'll be there well before dawn.'

'Let's get going then!' As he began walking again, Archie could hear a definite a squeak coming from his front legs. In fact, he was finding it harder to move. He tried to ignore the squeak, but Flo and Sparky could hear it too and they looked concerned.

'Don't look so worried,' said Archie. 'It's nothing that a few drops of oil won't sort out later.' But he failed to hide a wince of pain as he set off.

Flo was right, it only took them half an hour to arrive at what they hoped would be their new home.

'It's just over that wall,' said Flo. 'Take a look.'

Sparky zipped up the wall to see what Flo was pointing at.

'It's brilliant, Archie!' he said. 'You have to see!' Archie stretched his extendable neck as far as it would go. He could just see over the top of the wall. His eyes lit up when he saw the little attic window. He was so happy he could have cried – if robots could cry, of course.

'How do we get in?' he asked.

'There's a gate around the front,' said Flo.

'Well, what are we waiting for?!' said Archie. Then a look of panic came over his face. 'Aargh!'

'What is it?' asked Flo.

'I'm stuck! My neck! It won't go down!' His head swayed a bit in the wind. 'Help! It's a disaster! I don't want to be a giraffe!'

'What can we do?' said Flo, beginning to panic.

'Try and push my head down from the top!' suggested Archie.

Sparky and Flo jumped up and down on the top of Archie's head. It didn't budge.

'Wait,' said Archie, 'there's some oil in the sidecar. Flo, see if you can find it.'

While Flo went in search of oil, Sparky continued to jump up and down with as much force as his little body could muster.

'It's no good,' said Archie, panicking even more now. 'I'm doomed!'

Flo returned with the oil. 'Keep calm!' she said, not very calmly. 'We'll get you down.' Flo moved around Archie's head, spraying a little bit of the lubricating oil here and there where Archie's neck joined his head. 'Any better?' she asked.

'Does it look like it?' asked Archie. 'It's that rain – I'm probably beginning to rust.'

'Give it a minute to work its way in,' said Flo. She was trying her hardest not to sound as worried as she felt.

'Let's give the jumping one more go,' suggested Sparky.

'Go on then,' said Archie, convinced he was stuck with a two-metre long neck forever.

Flo and
Sparky jumped
up and down
for all they
were worth.
It seemed
hopeless,
then suddenly
Archie's neck
went back to

its normal length. It moved so fast that it caught
them all by surprise, and they ended up in a heap on
the pavement.

'Phew,' said Archie. 'That was scary.'

'Come on,' said Sparky. 'Let's find a way in
before you seize up completely! Once we're
inside you can have an oil bath if you need one!'

Chapter 10

Home At Last?

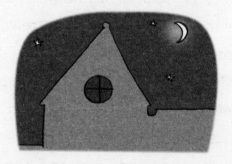

Around the front of the building, there was a metal fence with a gate in the middle. Archie stopped by the gate.

'It's got a keypad lock,' said Archie. 'Are you sure this place is empty?'

'Yes,' said Flo. 'There's no one here. The attic was just full of dust and cobwebs and a few old boxes.'

'We've nowhere else to go so we may as well give it a try,' said Archie.

'Can you get us in?' asked Sparky.

'No problem,' said Archie. He unscrewed the top panel of the keypad with the screwdriver in his paw, revealing the printed circuit board inside. He placed another paw gently on top of it, and connected to the circuit. 'Just need to hack in.' He closed his eyes to concentrate. 'A-ha!'

Archie disconnected, replaced the panel, pressed a sequence of numbers and the gate began to open.

'This is so exciting!' said Flo.

The Petbots pulled their sidecar through the gate and up to the front entrance. There was another keypad like the one that had opened the gate.

'This place can't be empty,' said Archie, puzzled,

as he hacked in again, 'not with all this security.'

'Let's just find the attic,' said Flo. 'I'm so tired, and I can't face another night outside.'

'No,' said Archie, 'I can't either.' He was worn out and still creaking from the wet night before.

It was completely dark inside the building. Archie lit up the hallway with his torchlight eyes and they spotted a staircase.

'Up there,' he said.

It was a bit of a struggle to get the sidecar up the stairs, but with some of grunting and groaning, three flights later, the stairs stopped at a large landing.

'Look!' said Flo. 'There's a hatch in the ceiling.' She flew up without a moment's hesitation and pulled at the handle with her beak.

The hatch opened and a ladder descended. Despite their exhaustion, there was a mad dash to get up into the attic room. Flo, having wings, had the advantage and flew through first.

'It's just like home!' she said.

It was uncanny.

The room was a slightly different shape, it was true, but at one end was a round window almost identical to the Professor's. There were a few old, age-stained boxes, mostly around the hatch

opening, and as Flo had said, judging by the layers of dust and the hundreds of cobwebs, no one had been up there for years.

Archie couldn't believe it. It looked like they'd had some luck at last.

'You're right, Flo,' he said wistfully. 'It's perfect. Quick, let's get the sidecar up here.'

'Can't we do it tomorrow?' pleaded Flo. 'I'm so tired.'

'Just to be on the safe side,' said Archie. 'I think it's best.'

It wasn't easy to winch the sidecar up through the narrow opening and it took almost every bar of their remaining charge. Eventually though, they moved it into the attic and pulled the ladder up behind them. Exhausted and happy, and feeling the safest they had for days, the Petbots settled down by the window and went to sleep.

When dawn broke, a shaft of warm sunlight came through the window, hit their solar panels and their batteries began to recharge.

'Hmmm, lovely!' said Archie, stretching and yawning. He lay back, contentedly resting on one of the old boxes and just soaking up the sunlight.

Flo was busy making herself at home. She'd begun to unload the knick-knacks she'd brought from the house. The first thing she did was to knock a nail into a rafter and hang a photo  of the Professor on it. Then she took out the bit of houseplant she'd brought and put it in the sunlight near the window.

Sparky was happily whizzing here and there, zooming up and down the beams as if they were racetracks and checking out every corner of the room. He zoomed through the clouds of dust that Flo was sweeping up with her wings.

After a while of watching all the feverish activity, Archie began to get curious. 'I wonder what's in those boxes,' he thought. 'Might be something useful.' The first box was just full of paper, the second contained an old globe. Archie looked at the date on the box. '1942 – positively ancient!' he laughed. He looked in another. That one was full of old pens, the kind people used to dip in ink wells. There was a second box of paper and another full of old history books.

That was when he realised he could hear sounds coming from outside. It was chattering and laughter – children's laughter. Archie's primary circuits suddenly made all sorts of connections with his memory banks.

'I know where we are,' he said. 'It's a —'

'School!' said Flo and Sparky, finishing his sentence as they peered out the window.

Archie ran over to join them. They looked out

to see hoards of schoolchildren coming through the open gates.

'That explains a lot!' said Archie. 'No wonder it's empty at night . . . and has the keypads! I should have realised.'

'Please don't tell me it means we have to leave?' Flo said with panic in her voice. 'I can't! I won't! I love it here! It feels like home already.'

'I agree with Flo. Please don't make us go,' moaned Sparky.

'But someone's sure to find us eventually,' said Archie, 'and then who knows what would happen to us?'

'I don't care,' Flo sulked. 'I want to stay.'

BBBRRRRIIIINNNGGGG!

The school bell rang, calling the children to their classrooms, and made the Petbots jump.

They heard the thunder of feet as the children filled the classrooms directly under them.

The Petbots froze, anxious not to make a single noise that might give them away.

BBRRINNG!

'Sparky,' whispered Archie, 'make a little hole in the ceiling with your laser. Be careful, though!'

While Sparky made the hole, Archie went to the sidecar and got out the laptop and spy camera. Then he pushed the camera into the hole and plugged the other end into the laptop. Instantly they had a view of the classroom below. Archie tuned in his ears, and played it for the other Petbots to hear.

'Did you do the homework, Sophie?' a boy whispered to the girl sitting next to him.

'Yes, Jack. Didn't you?' Sophie whispered back.

'Couldn't make head or tail of it,' he said. 'I hate fractions.'

'Me too,' said a girl sitting opposite them.

'But at least you can do them, Anya,' Jack groaned. 'I was hoping you and Sophie'd help me do it at break.'

'Quiet, please, class!' said the teacher. 'I'm coming round to collect your fraction homework.'

'Oops,' said Jack.

The Petbots watched the teacher collecting exercise books. When she reached Jack's table she was clearly unimpressed.

'Really, Jack, that's the third time this term you've not done your maths homework. You'll have to stay in the classroom after school and finish it instead of going to the Year Five art club.'

'But, Mrs Kinsey, I —' pleaded Jack.

'I'm sorry, Jack,' she said, 'but I need to know you've understood it.'

Jack sighed.

Flo saw the expression on the boy's face. 'Poor, Jack,' she said.

Archie looked at Flo and smiled. 'You're such a softy, Flo, you don't even know him,' said Archie.

'No, I know, but he looks so sad,' she said.

The teacher spoke to the rest of the class. 'And while I think about it, I need two volunteers to take down the summer holidays display during art club. We need to make room for our new topic – the Victorians!'

There was a collective groan from the class, but the two girls on the same table as Jack shot their hands into the air.

Sophie nudged Jack. 'We'll be here to help you out if you need us,' she said.

'Thanks!' Jack grinned.

'Thank you, girls,' said their teacher. 'Remember, though, be very careful not to touch the head teacher's magnificent model of the Eiffel Tower.'

As Mrs Kinsey collected the rest of the books, Archie zoomed in to the display in the corner of the classroom.

'Wow, that's impressive!' he said. There, on a

table near the window, stood a large model of the Eiffel Tower made entirely out of matchsticks. 'It must have taken him *ages.*'

'He'll be collecting it himself after art club,' Mrs Kinsey said. 'At about four o'clock.'

'*Four o'clock?!*' squeaked Sparky. 'How is anyone meant to stay quiet for that long?'

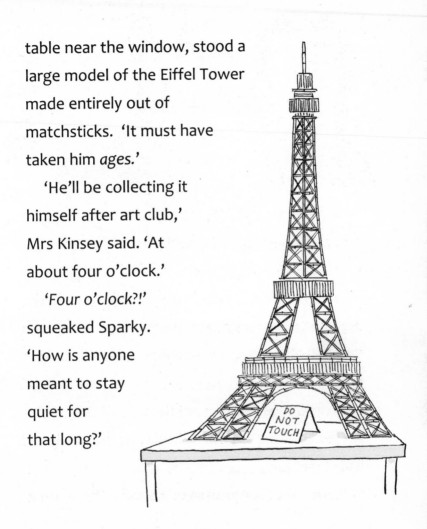

DO NOT TOUCH

Chapter 11

Discovered

'What are we going to do?' asked Flo. The Petbots had switched to their internal communications to make sure no one in the classroom heard them speaking.

'I really don't know,' said Archie, 'but I don't really see how we can make a new home here. We'll be discovered at some point.'

'But there are only people here in the day – and there are loads of school holidays,' said Flo.

'Yes, but it still means we'll be stuck up here all day and won't be able to move or make any noise.'

She was obviously upset. So was Sparky.

'I don't want to move any more than you, Flo,' said Archie. 'When everyone's gone home we'll take a proper look around the place and see if there's any way we could make it work.'

This made Flo a little happier. But the day still seemed to drag on endlessly. They gazed out of the window and watched the first few leaves of autumn blowing around the playground. Eventually the bell rang for the end of school, but still the three Year Five pupils remained in the classroom below.

'Jack, work quietly at your table while Anya

and Sophie take down the display. Leave your book on my desk and I'll mark it in the morning.'

'Yes, Mrs Kinsey.'

'Come over to the art room to let me know you've all finished before you go home.'

Archie watched on the laptop as the children went about their tasks. Flo was keeping herself busy dusting, and moving some of the smaller boxes into a neat pile.

'Careful, Flo,' said Archie, 'they might hear you.'

'I have to do something,' she said. 'I'm just feeling so nervous.'

In the classroom, the children were oblivious to what was going on above.

'It stinks in here,' said Jack as soon as Mrs Kinsey left the room.

'Doesn't it?' winced Anya. 'Apparently Robbie had a curry last night. He's been making a stink all day.'

'Nice of him to leave us a parting gift,' said Sophie, heading over to the window. 'I think we need some fresh air!' She opened the window and then she and Anya carried on taking down the display as Jack did his fractions.

'I'm actually getting this at last,' he said. 'It's not really that hard. I've nearly finished already. I'll give you two a hand in a minute.'

The girls smiled.

'So you're not totally useless then,' Sophie chuckled.

Just then, a gust of wind blew in the open window and the pile of papers that Sophie and Anya had carefully taken down blew all over the place.

'Oh no!' said Sophie, chasing the papers.

In the attic, the same gust of wind blew through the rafters, taking Flo completely by surprise – and off balance.

'Ohhhh!' she wailed as the gust caught her outstretched wings and threw her into the pile of boxes.

Archie didn't want to watch. He knew exactly what was going to happen, but was unable to look away. The boxes tumbled directly onto the hatch, pushing the ladder down. Flo went with it, crash-landing in a heap at the bottom!

'What on earth was that?' exclaimed Jack.

Jack, Anya and Sophie ran out of the classroom to see what had happened. Archie and Sparky were standing by the hatch looking

down. Flo tried to untangle herself from the boxes and their contents. She was frantic to get back in the loft before the children saw her.

But it was too late.

Jack, Sophie and Anya looked right at her, and then up at the open hatch. For a split second, the children's and the Petbots' eyes met. Then Flo

flew up and disappeared back inside, instantly followed by Archie and Sparky.

'Did you see them?!' said Anya, staring wide-eyed at the others.

Jack and Sophie nodded, speechless.

Then Jack ran for the ladder and Sophie and Anya followed.

'Er, hello!' said Jack, looking up at the hatch. 'Is anybody there?'

There was silence.

'What do you think?' said Jack. 'Should we go up and take a look?'

'Just try and stop me,' said Sophie, and marched straight past him, up the ladder into the dusty attic. 'Hello!' she said. 'Can you hear me?'

The Petbots were hiding behind the remaining boxes, still as statues, hoping desperately that the children would get bored and leave. They powered down completely in an attempt to seem lifeless.

'I didn't know this room was here,' said Anya.

'Me neither,' said Jack. 'What a cool place.'

'It's a bit dirty.' Sophie could feel her nose filling up with dust. They crept quietly around the attic until Sophie spotted where the Petbots were hiding. She nudged Anya. 'Look,' she whispered, 'over there.'

They walked slowly towards the strange-looking creatures.

'What are they?' asked Anya.

'I don't know,' said Jack. 'They look like they're made of metal.' He moved over, bent down and went to pick up Sparky. As he did, Sparky panicked, powered up and darted to the other side of the attic, leaving a trail of sparks behind him.

Jack fell over backwards, almost landing on Flo.

'Aaargh!' she shrieked, and flew up into the rafters.

Archie turned to look at them. His eyes powered up and glowed green. He shook his head in resignation and turned to the children.

'Looks like we'd better introduce ourselves,' he said. 'I'm Archie. That's Flo up there, and this,' he said, as Sparky returned to Archie's side 'is Sparky. We're Petbots.'

Archie went on to explain how they'd come to be hiding in the attic and about their quest to find a new home.

'I suppose we'll be moving on again now,' he said sadly. 'It's a shame though. This place was perfect for us. But the Professor always warned us that we must stay hidden from people because they'll dismantle us to see how we work and never be able to put us back together again.'

'Dismantle you?!' exclaimed Anya. 'Oh, that's awful.'

'But *we're* not people,' said Jack. 'Well, obviously we're people, but we're children not grown-ups. We'd never do that to you. It would be like . . . murder!'

'Jack's right,' said Sophie. 'Stay here! We can help you stay safe.'

'Yes,' agreed Anya. 'It would be horrible if you had to move again.'

'We'll keep your secret. It'll be fine. We promise,' added Jack.

The Petbots looked at each other.

'What do you think, guys?' said Archie.

Chapter 12

Sticking Together

'Oh please, let's stay,' begged Flo.

'Pleeeease!' said Sparky.

Archie tilted his head to one side. Could they really trust these children? He looked solemnly at Sophie, Jack and Anya.

'Well,' he said. 'We'll —'

Suddenly another huge gust of wind raced

through the window. It blew dust and cobwebs all over the attic.

CCRRASSHHH!

The noise came from the classroom below.

The children looked at each other, they all had the same bad feeling about the cause.

'I hope that wasn't what I thought it was,' said Anya nervously.

Archie turned the laptop towards them. 'Er . . . I'm afraid it was,' he said.

'It's a disaster!' said Sophie. 'What are we going to do? It's the head teacher's pride and joy!'

'We're dead!' groaned Jack. 'They'll never believe it was an accident!'

Anya burst into tears.

'Don't worry,' said Archie. 'It'll be okay.'

'What do you mean? How can it be okay? The whole classroom is covered in matchsticks!' wailed Anya.

'Trust me.' Archie grinned. 'We've had much bigger messes than this to sort out, including the odd exploding invention! Sparky, turbo speed. You know what to do.'

Sparky zoomed off, and Archie, Flo and the children went down to the classroom. There, they saw Sparky whizzing around the room, collecting up the matchsticks in his mouth.

'Bring them over here, Sparky,' said Archie, who was picking up the remains of the model. There wasn't much left intact. 'Glue, please.'

'I'll get it,' said Jack, heading for the stationary cupboard.

'Flo, can you bring up a picture of what it should look like?'

'Certainly.' Flo immediately projected an image of the model before it had been wrecked by the wind.

'Right, let's see,' said Archie, examining the construction in fine detail.

'Hey!' Sophie said to her friends. 'We'd better clear up the stuff in the hallway before Mrs Kinsey gets back, otherwise she'll know someone's up there.'

'Good idea!' said Jack.

'Excellent! Now for the fun,' said Archie. His eyes glinted, and with incredible speed he began to reconstruct the Eiffel Tower, matchstick by matchstick, exactly how it had been before the disaster.

When the boxes had been cleared up into the attic, and everything was back to normal, the children rushed into the classroom. They stared open-mouthed. They couldn't believe what they were seeing.

Archie was about two-thirds through the construction and Sparky had collected nearly all the matchsticks.

'Oh no!' said Sophie, crossing over to the window. 'Mrs Kinsey's on her way over.'

Anya gulped. 'And she's bringing the Head with her!'

'Uh-oh,' said Jack. The Eiffel Tower was growing before their very eyes but none of them knew whether Archie would finish in time.

They could hear the teachers' footsteps and their conversation as they entered the building.

'Yes, well, there are actually 10,342 matchsticks in total, you know, Mrs Kinsey.'

'Really, Headmaster, that's amazing.'

Archie had nearly finished rebuilding the Eiffel Tower. 'Flo, you and Sparky go back up to the attic,' he said quietly. 'This is going to be close.'

Flo looked reluctant. 'But what if they see you?'

'Go!' said Archie firmly.

The footsteps were getting nearer.

'And you know,' continued the head teacher, 'I think it's quite the best thing I've ever made.'

'It is lovely,' Mrs Kinsey grovelled.

'Nearly done,' said Archie, his paws a blur.

The teachers were approaching the final set of stairs.

The children exchanged glances.

Jack acted quickly to give Archie time to finish. He dashed out of the classroom and ran down the stairs, deliberately tripping up and ending in a heap at the bottom.

'Oopsie!' he said. 'Silly me!'

The Head glowered. 'Jack Robinson, there is a reason you are told not to run in school and you have just demonstrated what it is.'

'Sorry, sir.' Jack smiled stupidly.

'Get up, boy, and sort yourself out.'

Jack did as he was told and trudged up the stairs in front of the teachers to slow them down.

Back in the classroom, Archie was just finishing.

'There, last one! Over to you,' Archie said and sped out of the room and up the ladder, pulling it up behind him just as Jack and the teachers appeared at the top of the stairs.

Sophie and Anya stood in front of the matchstick model, grinning like idiots.

'Ah, admiring my model, I see!' said the Head, puffing his chest out proudly.

'Er, yes, sir. It's, um, amazing!' said Anya.

'We've finished everything, Mrs Kinsey,' said
Sophie, swiftly snatching the glue from the table
and hiding it behind her back.

'Thank you, Sophie. See you tomorrow, children.'

Sophie, Anya and Jack grabbed their bags and left the classroom.

In the hallway, they spotted the Petbots peering through a crack in the hatch. Archie winked. The children giggled, gave a sneaky thumbs up in return, and ran down the stairs.

Archie quietly closed the hatch. 'Phew!' he said. 'That was intense!'

Flo watched the children walk across the playground. 'Aren't they nice?' she said.

'Yes,' agreed Sparky. 'I really liked them.'

Archie joined Flo and Sparky at the window.

'So, do you think we can we stay?' asked Flo.
Sparky looked up hopefully.

Archie smiled. 'Yes,' he said, 'I think we can.'

'Hooray!' Flo and Sparky cheered together.

'I feel at home already!' said Flo, doing a celebratory swoop around the attic.

'Me too!' said Sparky, zooming around and filling the air with his sparks.

Archie smiled. He walked over to the photo of the Professor that Flo had hung on the rafters earlier.

'Well, Professor,' he said, 'I think we'll be all right after all.'

Coming soon

PETB🐾TS

JUDY BROWN

School Shutdown

The Petbots are settling into their new home in a
school, sneaking around at night and
having fun with their human friends
Jake, Anya and Sophie.

When Jake crashes a school computer, he's happy
he has Archie around to get it working again!

But afterwards, Archie starts to act strangely, and no
repairs that Flo and Sparky make can stop him
malfunctioning. He's caught a computer virus!

The schoolchildren and Petbots must team up
to find a cure before Archie
shuts down forever!

**Trace the components
in different combinations to create
your very own Petbots!**

Head online to

petbots.co.uk

for more fun and games!